FULLMOON CLASSICS
THE HOUSE OF A BROKEN SHADOW
"Fictitious Horror"
She might know where you are. She might follow you till you die"
A GHOST STORY
A SHARMA

A SHARMA

THE HOUSE OF A BROKEN SHADOW

A Ghost Story

Fullmoon Classics

FullMoon Classics Books

FullMoon Classics Books is an imprint of
A SHARMA.

Publication Data

Names: A Sharma, author.

Title: The house of a broken shadow / A Sharma.

Description: FullMoon Classics Books.

[2020] Summary: Told in one voice. Isabella. A girl with her curse. Cursed by a witch, a veiled ghost, appears in her dreams every night. It follows her. And it'll follow her, till her death. Why did she get cursed? Is it her legacy or destiny or what?

Subjects: CYAC: Ghosts—Fiction. |Friendship—Fiction. | Extrasensory perception—Fiction. | Fate and fatalism—Fiction. | Haunted houses—Fiction. | Family life—West Virginia—Fiction. | Huntington—Fiction. |

For my parents and friends for supporting my love of books.

Fullmoon Classics

AN IMPRINT OF A SHARMA

TABLE OF CONTENTS

INTRODUCTION

There is a lot of mythology and folklore about the witch who collects demons and souls. Between cultures and times, there is always a fear of stealing souls. Soul collectors consume the soul in various ways. Eating them usually leads to death or becomes an empty shell. Essentially all witchcraft can be seen as gathering souls. Dealing with spirits is one of the two main practices of witchcraft.

Witches were considered evil beings. The early witches were those who practiced witchcraft, used magic spells and asked spirits to help or bring change. Most witches were considered pagans who worked as devils. Many, however, were only natural healers or so-called "intelligent women", whose choice of profession was misunderstood.

Witchcraft commonly associated with people who use metaphysics to harm innocent people. Witchcraft was generally evil and often associated with Satan and Satan worship. This led to death, torture, blamed for misfortune, and many years of rampant witch-trials and witch hunts.

STORYLINE

If you find an empty house alone in the woods, you probably would like to cast-off the thoughts of going inside. But if you want to explore the chilling dread environment and empty dark rooms of that house or have much courage to find who's living in that house since those preceding years, you would step ahead.

"I never summoned up my courage to this level before. Never ever tried to confront an evil spirit or thought about it. Nonetheless, I never dreamed of anything demonic. We never want to forget the past of our lives, unless it's a bad one. Everything depends on what we did or what really happened back then.

My past was a little horrifying I would say. I can't forget it, even if I want to. I tried everything to erase it from my mind, but I failed as always. Those days still haunts me. And when I remember those days, my blood runs cold".

Hello, my name is Isabella. And this is my story.

CHAPTER 1
THE COLLATION

Huntington, West Virginia 1891.

Okay, calm down. See. There it is. There's the house. Now listen to me. Whatever would happen there, whatever you see, in that house, just don't go for it, okay? Just stick together. Stick together or die alone. We don't know what's lurking inside that house" "Adam said"

"But I don't want to go in there. In that house. I know there's a ghost, waiting. It wants our soul. All of our soul. I can feel it" "John said with a scared voice"

"Listen to me, John. We got our friend trapped inside that house. We all saw him following to something. Something imperceptible to us. You could tell him sleepwalking. But make no sense to me. He wasn't him. It was something else.

Someone must have summoned him. And we have to try at least once. I'm not a coward. Not even you. So, act like a brave one" "Adam said"

"What will we do if we saw something terrible, inside" "Luke frowned"

"Then don't react to that. We can't leave him alone, starving and dying. As I said, stick together no matter what" "Adam answered"

"Who's at the window, Adam?" "John asked"

Adam looked towards the house and someone just walked beside the window. Waiting for them to come over.

"I saw a black figure staring at us" "John repeated"

"Shh, don't make any noise. It could be the person behind it. Follow me. I know the directions. There should be his footsteps leading all the way inside. We'll follow the same" "Adam said"

As they walked near to the house, a cold breeze sensation got them shivered from nowhere. And as closer they were coming, the colder it was running. They could now feel someone's presence there. They could feel something cold like an evil spirit around them.

As Adan opened the door, the house was all dark inside. Empty like a rat cage waiting for its prey to be trapped there.

And that was the moment when John saw a glimpse of a girl going downstairs.

“Adam, I think I saw someone” “John said”

“Who? Sam?” “Adam asked”

“No. I don’t think so. It looked like a girl trying to say “follow me.” I think she wants to show us the way to Sam” “John answered”

“Como on let’s go fast. We have to find him” “Luke said and drove his legs fast forward”

“Luke, together” “John said”

When they headed downstairs, they saw no one except their friend lying on the ground.

“See, there he is” “Luke answered”

“Sam. Sam, wake up. Look, we're here for you. We’re here to take you back home. Come on, get up” “Luke said when he was trying to wake him up”

“Why he isn’t responding” “John asked”

“Oh, my lord, look at his face. He’s dead” “Adam answered when he saw his face”

“Shut up. He’s gonna wake up” “John interrupted”

“Uh, guys! What’s that?” “John asked when he turned around his eyes to take a look around”

“Where? “Adam asked”

“There, in the corner of our left” “John answered”

“John, there’s no one” “Adam answered”

“Who are you? How do you know my name?” “John whispered to someone invisible”

“John? Who are you talking to?” “Adam asked”

“She’s asking me to come over” “John answered”

“Who?” “Adam asked”

“The girl in the corner. I can see her” “John answered”

“She’s crying ‘help me’. I think she’s also been trapped here. I’m going to help her” “John answered”

“John. John wait. We’re not here to die. Whatever it is, don’t go for it. John, john…” “Adam said and ran after him”

And when Adam approached to him, he saw someone was already there. But it wasn’t a girl at all. It was a lady. And John was on the ground. Dead. And now she twisted her head towards Adam.

Adam saw her burnt face and black eyes. He had no option rather than to run. He ran. Ran as fast as he could to reach back to Luke.

“Luke come on. We have to go now. Come on” “Adam said”

As hurriedly Luke stood up and tried to run away after, he just got numbed within a trace of the moment, as if someone has clenched his body. She was there, behind him now. She inhaled his soul within blink of an eye, and threw him empty a few distances away on the floor.

“No. no…

Adam started to run back when she whispered…

“Where are you going? You can’t run from me. I’m a heartless in power here. There’s no escape, no way back home”

“It's so satisfying, watching you beg on your knees, oh my”

Now he was on the floor too. And she turned herself back into the house. Calm and satisfied. “And the door, the door that she always leaves closed”

CHAPTER 2
ISABELLA LARSSON

Harrisonburg, Virginia 1911.

She could sense the spirit energy or the negative energy around her. Every time she looks into the dark woods, she always feels the presence of someone hiding and walking behind those dense trees. Her voice was quiet. But since it came unexpectedly at her through the darkness of her room, it nearly made her scream. She was in bed, staring at the moon out the window and still worrying about what tomorrow would be like.

A breeze blew from the woods, and she heard a noise that sent another wave of chills down her back. She stopped what she was doing and looked into those dense trees one more time. Something was walking. Walking with the most silence steps it could make. But the dead leaves were upsetting her silence. Then it stopped. She tried to focus her eyes on to that as much as she could. Then she realised something. Whatever it was, it was staring at her, from the woods. It looked like a lady or a woman, and she was continuously staring at her. But it was a pretty dark night outside, so she couldn't clearly identify her.

"What are you looking at?" "Anna asked"

"Did you hear that?" "Isabella asked her"

"What?" "Her mother looked outside through the window"

"There's Nothing. Come on, let's get this window closed" "Anna said"

"I didn't want to open it. But I heard a voice... I swear I heard a woman laughing" "Isabella said"

"You were supposed to be asleep. You had to go to the hostel in the morning, remembered? You have already talked about your bad dreams with me" "Anna said"

"It was not a dream. I haven't even fallen asleep yet" "Isabella shout"

"We'd had that talk too. Sometimes when you dream something over and over again, then our mind starts playing tricks on us. You think you're not dreaming, but that still isn't real" "Anna answered"

“I know, you have a hard time distinguishing reality from dreams. I was just like you, at your age, but I didn't believe it. You're seventeen years old. You're too big for bad dreams” “Anna said”

“I wasn't dreaming!” “Isabella yelled”

“Now you learn to shout on me, young girl”? (Anna yelled after she uncovered her ears)

“I said I wasn't dreaming. I heard something from the woods. That made me sit up straighter” “Isabella whispered”

“I had watched enough horror documentaries and I know that a lot of animals woke up at night to hunt, especially in the forest. The noises are natural. Even if they are scary, they're just animals. And they are not coming to my room anyway. But I can make a difference. I know what are dreams and what are real. I'm not talking to you in my dreams right now, at least” “Isabella said”

“Are you sure you weren't asleep?” “Anna asked”

“No, it wasn't a dream” “Isabella shook her head no”

“But mom I know that last night, it was a dream, not really happened. I knew, that it was a bad dream because I wouldn't have walked into the woods on my own foot at night anyway” “Isabella said”

“Okay, just take a healthy sleep. You will be fine” “Anna said”

"Yeah, hope so. I have to pack my stuff. Than to sleep. Good night, mom" "Isabella said"

"Good night, sweetie. Make it quick" "Anna replied"

"I used to have horrible dreams since my childhood about lots of people are running from something cruel. Trying to escape their death from something bizarre. I used to see a witch in my dreams. The same witch in every dream to be exact, calling my name and convincing me to go with her. Like she knows me. Every time I see her in my dreams, she used to say the same thing over and over to me, like, 'You belong to me', 'come to me, let me take your soul to peace". But every time I discussed it with my parents, they just cheered me saying 'It's just a dream, forget it". But I know there's nothing they can do about that. But it was like I'm living in some kind of constant fear. Like someone is waiting for me. And it going to find me one day. My dreams were mystifying but meaningless to me.

CHAPTER 3
THE DREAM

One night, I was in the forest. Still ... I could hear the howl of the distant wind. I could taste the fear in my throat as I walked. I didn't know why I was dreaming of the woods. I didn't know why I wasn't waking up. I just knew I had to keep walking.

If I stopped walking, she would find me".

"If she finds me, I would die".

The woods were dark but the moon above was full, so I could see the faint path below my feet. Maybe I should go to a different way.

But no, if I did that, I'd get lost, and then she'd definitely find me, and I would definitely be dead.

I had to keep moving. Had to stay warm.

I had to find ... something. But what?

Keep walking. Keep walking.

Something snapped behind me. I turned around. My heart was beating so loud and fast, I could hear it clear within all the silence I had. A shadow moved between the trees. The flash of glowing white eyes.

I ran.

I ran, and it ran after me.

I could hear it now, crashing through the trees. Calling out. Calling my name.

"***Isabella... Isabella...***" It was getting closer. I ran faster. Branches tore at my legs and hit my face, but I didn't stop.

It was so close. I could hear its breath. I could feel its breath.

Up ahead.

Through the trees.

There was a light. A window. A house.

It would be my house. Once I poach to my house, it would keep me safe. I ran harder, and the creature behind me was howling now, howling and laughing. Laughing like an old woman.

I was running, and running. I was so close to home.

But when I passed through the trees, I knew I was wrong. It wasn't my house. It was an old house. The yard was overgrown and filled with weeds. But I didn't have time to care. I ran up the path up to the front door. The lights were on. Someone had to be home. I pounded on the front door.

"Please!" I yelled. *"Please let me in! She's coming for me! Please, help!"*

A shadow moved behind the curtain. The creature howled behind me.

The door opened.

I looked at the person who opened it ... and it wasn't a person at all. It was a lady. A lady in the Veil.

Slander and tall, very tall with a black veil on her face.

"*Welcome Home, Isabella*," she said.

Before I could scream, before I could run, the lady's cold fingers wrapped around my wrist, and she yanked me inside and threw me outside from the back door. I was on the ground.

Now she was hovering up in the air…. I saw the house right below her. That house was the only house, alone in that forest. I tried to get up, but my body wasn't in control of myself anymore. She was controlling me with her power, kind of a witch power. I could feel that power.

And now, she lifted her body down all of a sudden. Now she was on the ground and right in front of me, possessing me. I still wasn't able to move my legs, my hands, my body. Her face was covered. She doesn't allow anyone to see her face.

She wanted to eat my soul. I was looking at my worst nightmare. Her hungry eyes were flaming, flashing out from her veil. Her veil slithered away from her face just for a moment with a gust of wind, and I saw her cruel burnt face. A face of the devil. Hungry for my soul. Wanted to take all of the pure soul I had.

“Why are you afraid of me, don't worry I won't hurt you. I just need your soul. You know you can do nothing in front of me. I'm much more powerful and tall" “The lady in the Veil”

“Please let me go…please" “I screamed out loud”

“Ha-ha… You, you belong to me” “The lady in the Veil”

And now she opened her mouth.

She opened her mouth so big that it could have perhaps swallow a whole human head. And now she attacked… and I woke up.

It was 8 of the morning.

“Oh, the same nightmare, again” “Isabella whispered”

“You look like you didn't sleep well” “my mom said at breakfast”

“Yes, I... I did,” “I said”

I didn't want to repeat my nightmare with my mother. My mom was stressed out enough already. She didn't need anything else on her mind.

“You had bad dreams.” “Mom asked”

“No, I didn't!” “I nodded my head no”

But Mom clearly didn’t believe me. She walked over and gave me a back hug to my neck. And said,

“Oh, honey. Everyone has bad dreams. I didn't want to tell you that I was having bad dreams too when I was at your age. Neither of them needed to know. I just want you to promise me one thing,” “Mom said”

“What?” “I asked”

“Whatever you do, don't go into the woods” “Anna replied”

“What's so dangerous about the woods, anyway? They're beautiful” “I Asked”

“Beauty can hide great evil. The woods are deep, and she is hungry. And if she has her way, she’s gonna take you away from me”

“Who is she? I wanted to know more” “Isabella asked”

It’s time to go. "Remember. Have you packed your stuff, your bag? “Anna asked”

“Of course, mom” “Isabella answered”

Let's finish your breakfast. Your taxi will be right here anytime” “Mom said”

“Look who’s here?” “Someone said to me”

“Ant Hadley” “I screamed and hugged her”

“Oh, my sweetheart. I heard you leaving today?” “Aunt Hadley asked”

“Yes, aunt Hadley. Did you see my backpack? It’s got a doll on it” “I said with my happy wide eyes”

“Oh, it’s so beautiful sweetheart” “Aunt Hadley replied”

“But promise me one thing that you are going to stay away from bad people. Bad people bring bad luck. So, no bad friends” “Aunt Hadley said”

“I promise you, Auntie” “I said and hugged her again”

Peep...peep, Taxi honked!

“Look taxi arrived” “Anna said”

“Yeah mom, I'm going” “I said with a sad smile”

I took my bag and hopped in the taxi.

“Goodbye mom. Say goodbye to dad. He always busy. Bye Auntie Hadley. I will miss you all. I love you all” “Isabella said when waving her hand”

“Goodbye honey. And take care, my doll” “Mom said with tears in her eyes” “Ahh, she’s strong. She’s a strong girl” “Aunt Hadley said and waved her hand back”.

CHAPTER 4
COME BACK HOME

Greensboro, Virginia 1912.

A year has been passed. Everything was going fluently and slightly touched by silence. Silence generally resembles the storm that is about to come. But how can be a story could be a story without anything fortuitous. Unpredictable and unimaginable happenings don't ask for the address. It always happens, when the time come. It could be worse. In fact, prayers can fail too. Sometimes God lets us travel through our darkest time, alone, so we can know the actual meaning of life and fear. Besides, he knows how strong we are, and how far we can go.

It was evening, me and all my friends were going for dinner. We're going to have winter holidays a few days later. Finally, we were about to go home. I was about to go home. And I was so excited about that. I was so excited to meet my mom and dad. It's been a long time since I saw their faces. We were not allowed to meet anyone until we pass our finals. And I was missing them, so much. Since I was in the hostel, I never dreamed of her. She stopped visiting me. I think she must've rested in peace, whoever she was. And I never felt anything strange like I used to. It could be the environment, or, or the place. Must be the place. Because the hostel was in the town. And my home, was in deep countryside, apart from the city. And most of all, nearest to a forest.

It was 8 in the evening when the warden came in front and said,
"There's a phone call for you"
"Who" "I questioned"
"From your home" "Warden answered"
That news made me smile, but not to the warden. She hasn't had a smile on her face. But I didn't care and run towards the warden's office to pick up the call. I went to the spot, where the telephone was.
"Hello, mom" "I picked up the phone and asked"
"Hello, Isabella" "A man answered, but it wasn't my dad"

“Who?” “I asked”

“We are calling you from central police department. This call is to inform you about your parents. They’re no more. They died last night” “Officer answered”

“What? Shut up. Who are you?” “I asked with fear”

“I'm detective. Detective Edward” “Man answered”

“My condolence, miss Larsson. We already have started our investigation, and we want you here. We have some questions for you” “Detective asked”

“Ok Detective, I’ll be there tomorrow, by the noon” “I answered with grief”

I couldn’t sleep and cried all night thinking about why and who killed them. But they weren’t with me anymore, and that was the most awful thing of my life.

The next morning, I took the first bus to my hometown. When I was there, I saw the house. Nothing was really wrong with the house. Everything was fine. Like nothing happened. No break-in. I started to check the house from outside because the house had been sealed all the way up. So, I went to the backyard. Again, nothing wrong. When I was checking, a cold sensation touched my ears. I turned around so quick and beheld. But nothing was there. Only the dark, dense and scary woods behind me as always. Then I started to feel like someone wants me to walk, to the forest. Like someone has been already waiting for me in there. All my fears were keep telling me not to go and my mind was asking, who's there? I didn't realise my feet shuffling all by itself. All I was hearing my mom calling my name.

But my mom's dead. Who's calling me than? Why I'm keep hearing her voice?

I have to check, at least. I have to keep walking, or I will lose her.

"Umm, miss Larsson?" "Someone called my name"

"Yes? Sorry, didn't see you coming. Did you say something?" "I asked"

"Where you going?" "Detective asked"

"I.... I just don't know, I just... I just checking" "I answered"

"I want to ask you a question" "Detective said"

"Have ever your parents told you about something. Like something that can harm them?" "Detective asked"

"What you mean?" "I asked"

"I mean if they have made some enemy?" "Detective answered"

"No, they never involved me between anything beyond my age" "I answered"

"Can I check my house officer?" "I asked"

“Yeah…yeah. Sure. But not today. Maybe tomorrow. Your house is still under investigation. We have called the forensic expert, so tomorrow? But don’t touch anything.” “Detective said”

“And one more thing, Mrs Hadley is here. She wants to see you” “Detective said”

“Can I see them. If I could see them one last time?” “I requested”

“Who?” “Detective asked”

“My parents. I want to see them” “I answered”

“Of course. And in addition of the investigation, we also want you there. Anything you can do, will help us, to find the murderer” “Detective said”

“Oh, here she is” “Detective said when he saw Mrs Hadley coming through”

“I’m so sorry, sweetheart” “Mrs Hadley came and hugged me”

“I started to cry on her shoulder”

“Come with me. Come. Thankyou Detective” “Aunt Hadley said”

“Not at all. The forensic experts arrived. What a timing” “Detective answered”

“Come sit here”

Aunt Hadley made me comfortable and went to the kitchen for a glass of water. Then she arrived and handed over to me.

"What happened to them, aunt Hadley." "I asked"

"I really know nothing about how this happened so quick. But that night something was there. Something I felt very awful" "Aunt Hadley answered"

"What… awful? "I asked"

"It was the night before yesterday, when I heard a scream. A loud scream. A scream that was as loud as a human lung can make. Me and my husband were sleeping when I heard it all. I ran to my window to check. Nothing. I rolled my eyes to your house if I could see your mother at the window. I thought she must've heard it too. The lights were off, like they never heard anything. So, I shook it off.

Yesterday morning I walked to your door, to talk to your mother about what happened last night. So, I knocked on the door. Didn't get any responses. I knocked again. No answer. Then I knocked again and again. Twenty times at least, but I got the same, no response. So, I circle around to your house, but were no sign of breaking in. The house was locked from inside and we heard only screams in the middle of the night. So, we called the police to investigate the house and check if they're okay. And I was so much devastated when police found them dead. I felt dead too" "Mrs Hadley said grieving"

“I don’t know where to stay now. The investigation is still going on.” “I asked”
“Let them do their work. Stay with me as long as you can. At least, till the investigation is going on. This is your house. And I am your aunt. You’re my girl now. And you’re safe here, with me. And I’m not letting you stay alone somewhere else” “Mrs Hadley said”
“Thank you so much Aunt Hadley” “I said and hugged her”

Trying to clear her mind, Isabella headed her house next morning. The old house was untouched. The furniture and the decor everything covered in a thin layer of dust. Isabella stood by the family portrait staring at her mother's family. As far as she knew her aunts and uncles were far older than her and probably dead by now, except Mrs. Hadley. She had never met any of her relatives. No sign of murderer. Nothing strange. Every corner, every room of the house was perfectly fine. Like nothing has ever happened at all. I was still in shock and my heart was pounding.

That night, it was raining. Aunt Hadley made her bed and she simply went to bed exhausted. Staring at the window speckled in raindrops, until she dozed off.

The Next Morning

When I woke up the next morning, it was still pouring. nonetheless, I got ready and headed to the hall.

"Aunt Hadley?" "I called"

"Yes, sweetheart" "Aunt Hadley answered"

"I use to have dreams. Nightmares about someone. A lady. I have never seen her my entire life. Sometimes I see a lady burning and screaming. It's almost like I'm... remembering it. Flashes of someone else's memories" "I said"

"Did she tell you, her name?" "Aunt Hadley asked"

"Never. Never I saw her face" "I answered"

"You see her, that means you're cursed" "Aunt Hadley made me unnerved"

"Aunt Hadley, please tell me anything you know. My mom never told me anything about it? All I knew was to stay away from those woods?" "I asked"

"There were seven old towns. centuries ago, deep in the countryside. And one of them was a curse upon them all. The black town. There was a girl named Diana who rapidly became a super witch unlike any other. But it came at a terrible price. Killing the people, the whole town, even the mind of herself. Diana's mother, Alana pleaded with her to stop using it before their world irrevocably damage. However, Diana resented her mother, thinking her own mother was trying to steal her power.

So, she resorted to dark magic and crafted a book of evil. The black book. She transformed herself into monster. So, the priests gathered and captured her, burnt her and imprisoned her remains and he black book with a spell cast with their own blood... to ensure that Diana's dark power would never be found. And that is why she has been stricken from the chronicles.

This evil was supposed to remain frozen for eternity. But someone might have freed her. And now it's slowly possessing you. But even with the powers, she still can't be freed. Priests used blood magic to steal her in her prison. Only those themself could release her completely who belongs to their bloodline. Or the last of their bloodline. That means she needs blood of you, because you're the end of the bloodline.

Through her agony, she cursed the entire village when she was burning. She said, she'll return for her vengeance and will slay each and every person and their descendants so far.

She'll eat their souls to satisfy the curse. And she will wander until no one's alive. And for this she has to complete her curse. She will eat your soul and use your blood to free herself completely, so she can be born once again. She'll live around you, wait for you.

And, when your time will come, she will consume you."

This was as far as I knew, sweetheart" "Aunt Hadley said"

The story made me even more scared as I was before. The same bloodline leads to the same curse, my grandma used to say that. And one has to pay the price. Most of the time we don't have the way out, but sometimes we do. We don't care, until the day it comes, to an end. And that's the time we realise whatever we did, whatever we thought, was a mistake.

CHAPTER 5
DIANA

Oh, I'm silent like a doll, but I can walk through the wall…
I can see you, even my eyes are burned at all...
You can't run from me oh I can roll like a ball…
I have no shadow, I'm much more powerful and tall…

Millwood, 1879.

Millwood, an isolated village deep in the countryside. It was a dark night when a girl born in a family. The first child. Born with the mark of unholiness. The mark of the devil, on back of her neck. The moment she was born, her parents felt mortified by her birth cause' they believed the girl derived bad luck to them.

She was devil's child, they believed. Malevolent. The unholiness in her eyes. She may be cursed, but how could something beautiful be awful? No one could tell. And they have to get through the situation no matter what is the cost. They can't kill her or dump her somewhere to die. She was their girl, how could they? They named her Diana.

When she grew up, the children of her age used to laugh at her, make fun of her when they see her around. Nobody liked her. Nobody wanted to talk to her, they believed that her presence around them could curse them too. Everyone called her a wretch of hell. She used to cry sometimes, alone at her house when she watches children playing, laughing, with each other. Because when she tries to join them, they all stop playing and run far away. Screaming *"Run, she's a witch"*. And that started to break her heart real fast.

Few years have been passed. She became 15. Now she did not want to go out. And she often caged herself down in her own house. The life of hatred no one would expect. She was alone and miserable. Out of smiles. A little plant that has never been watered with love and sympathy by anyone. But what was her fault though? Why she was treated like that? it wasn't her mistake! Not at all. She never asked a life like this. She was just a child, just a little girl. An innocent girl who just wanted to be loved and respect and the life like all those children around her. But she never got what she deserved, only pain and suffering. She was always looked upon with contempt and hatred, and all that damages changed that innocent heart completely into a malevolent. And one day she made a promise. A promise to herself, that the people who laughed at her, abused her, and called her a witch, would have to pay the price. The very first rage flourished inside of her. And now the seeds of hatred had been sown inside of her. She has now become ruthless.

"Diana?" "Her mom asked when she entered her room"

"Yes mother." "Diana answered"

"What are you doing?" "Her mother asked"

"Nothing… I was just drawing something" "Diana answered"

"Let see what you drew" "Mother said"

"Hmm, beautiful. How did you draw it?" "Mothe asked"

"I don't know, I just thought about it and..." "Diana answered"

"This is so beautiful" "Mother cheered her up"

"Really mother?" "Diana asked"

"Yes" "Mother answered"

"Okay. After when you finish all these beautiful drawings, can you bring some firewood. Your father will be here late today. And I need them for stove?" "Mother asked"

"But I don't want to go out" "Diana answered"

"But why?" "Mother asked"

"It makes me sad" "Diana answered"

"Oh, my little doll. They don't know about how precious you are. They only jealous of how someone can be so beautiful. So, they think that you probably have done some magic on yourself that's why you are so beautiful" "Mother said"

"Then why they all run away from me" "Diana asked"

"They run from you because they think if you come near to them, they would look uglier than they already are. Hahaha" "Mother answered"

"Really mother?" "Diana asked with a happy face"

"Yes. You're the most beautiful girl in the whole world. And you don't have to think about what people says. They're ugly pigs" "Mother said"

"Diana smiled and then laughed"

"Okay, get those branches before it gets dark outside" "Mother said"

"On my way, mother" "Diana answered"

She was at the main door when she saw everyone leaving. Hiding and peeking out. She had her mother's words, but she doesn't want to get sad again. She has smiled today and she doesn't want to spoil it. So, she preferred to get out when no one's playing out in her way. So, she doesn't have to face anyone and feel mortified by their words again.

She peeked one last time if all of them have cleared the path. The forest was towards the north of the village. It was dense and dark but no wild animals to harm. Diana's house was at the end, next to the forest. She made herself move and went inside of the forest. It was nearly sunset and she had to be quick. So, she was hurriedly collecting any firewood she was seeing. She had to be quick or her mother would be mad at her. As she was collecting, she noticed someone through the corner of her eyes. First, she scared then she turned over. She saw some people. Sitting in a circle.

1.. 2..3…. there was 9 of them.

She was wondering if she knew them. But they weren't the villagers she could count on. They were outsiders. And were praying to something together. So, she dared to get close to them and see what they were doing because it was almost dark. She started walking silent steps. As she stepped close to them, she saw, there were a bunch of dolls, human skulls, candles, etc.

They were practicing the black magic. In the middle of the forest.

One of them felt her presence…

"Go home. Little girl" "He said and interrupted the prayer"

"What are you all doing here? "Diana asked"

"This is not safe. Go home. It's already dark" "A man warned"

"First tell me what all of you are doing here or I'll tell everyone about you" "Diana said"

"This is witchcraft" "The man answered"

"But I heard witchcraft is for the devil" "Diana asked"

"Yes, sort of. But this will not cause any harm to any person of this village. This is for our own will" "The man replied"

"Can you help me to cure myself?" "Diana asked"

"Don't even dare to think about that, this is too dangerous" "The man warned her"

"If this is dangerous then why you're performing such type of things near to our home? You're not allowed to do these kinds of stuff here. It can affect us. This can lure bad luck to our home. Even the demons. So, tell me what I'm asking or I'm going to complain the priests about you all. And they gonna punish you with their own magical way" "Diana said"

"Okay fine, but girl, this is dangerous. you can't hold it by yourself alone. Still, you want to learn this?" "The man asked"

“I don’t care. Just tell me. can this thing cure me?” “Diana asked”

“Yes. But you have to worship the devil so the devil can offer you the things you have wished for. So, you have to follow all the steps carefully, even the slightest mistake can lead you to your sacrifice to whom you’re worshipping. We can only tell you the ways to learn it but we’re not staying here to teach you” “The man said”

“Okay. Just tell me the way” “Diana asked”

“You have to gather all these things on a sigil of Baphomet on that place where you want to perform this. You have to learn the actual meaning of witchcraft written in this book and you can do whatever you want. But be careful because it takes an offering in return for every gift it gives. You have to find someone who can teach you the dark secrets of black magic. Because self-learning will make your dark intentions to rise for more. But a teacher can teach you how to control it in a perfect way. You have to decide wisely. Seek a teacher with a bright mind who neglect dark ones.

“Here. Take this book, but don’t ever try to misuse it. This is really dangerous” “The man warned”

“What do you mean by dark minds?” “Diana asked”

“You will know, soon” “The man answered”

“There is a lady who used to do black magic once, now she lives alone in a dense forest pretty far from here. You may go to her, maybe she can help you. But keep in mind that she is a witch and has mastered in black magic. But she used that black magic for the good of the people. With this, you can cure yourself. But don’t be greedy for more or you’ll summon the devil himself. Black magic beats quickly, dominates you. Specially the one who is tempted. So, you should keep in mind that if you’re using black magic more than just to cure yourself, then you will have to bear the consequences” “The man said”

“Don’t worry, I will use black magic only to cure herself, nothing more” “Diana answered”

“You would hear lots of dreadful voices. It will take a whole day on foot to reach there. You should pack your essentials and walk onto that path as soon as the morning rises. Take some rest at a safe place at night before you enter ***‘the haunted forest’***. Carry a knife or some sharp thing with you for your safety like lanterns etc. and the most important thing...Don't panic...don’t be afraid”

The thought tucked inside her head.

That night

“Mother, can I ask you for a permission?” “Diana asked”
“For what” “Mother asked”
“I want to visit someone” “Diana answered”
“Who?” “Mother asked”
“A doctor” “Diana answered”
“But why? Are you ill?” “Mother asked”
“No. Today I met some people and they told me there’s a doctor who cures people’s permanent scars that doesn’t fade away” “Diana answered”
“But we can’t leave our house like that. Your father isn’t here for three days” “Mother answered”
“No, no need to leave the house abandoned. I’m going alone. It’s not too far. I’ll pack my essentials and stop somewhere when the sun goes down” “Diana said”
“How much time it’s gonna take you to come back” “Mother asked”
“Just two days and one night” “Diana answered”
“You are not in any kind of danger, right?” “Mother asked”
“No. Absolutely not, mother” “Diana answered”
“Okay than. Be here before your father come back” “Mother allowed her”
“Thank you so much mother” “Diana said”
“Okay. Let me help you pack your essentials. You must start your journey with the first light” “Mother said”

The next morning

She left the house as soon as the sun came up. She was so thrilled and excited. She was walking in the forest and fantasizing *'what it would be like if I can do magical things. Magical Diana.' 'She giggled'*

She has been walking for hours now but no house came in sight. She remembered the words that they told her that it's going to be a long, long way. The lady's house was 9 miles away from that village, which has to be done through that dreadful forest surrounded by trees. The forest was so dense that even the light could not brighten up the path she was been on to. Like all the sunlight has been reflecting through the forest itself. But she had no choice. It was more like she was granting her own wish. She was already being so crazy thinking about the results that had never been promised. She was moving, doesn't care about what was going to appear next to her.

Sun went down slowly and now she had the dark path ahead, '***The haunted forest***'. She was brave and nothing was going to stop her. The excitement of power, overlapped and she forgot about spending the night before entering the haunted forest. She had to go through that way but not in the dark. The only thing she remembered was the lady. She took out her flashlight and said… '*oh my, it's so very bright, I can see the road. Ha-ha.*'

And then, she stepped off into the forest.

As soon as she stepped inside, something gave her goosebumps. She heard someone saying *"**Who are you?**"*. It was a woman's voice. Chills ran through her spine. She didn't stop but it made her calm down. The darkness of the forest started to feed on her fears. She pondered how easy it would be to come lost and terrified out here or worse to disappear completely. How easy it would be to die off and how slim the chances of survival would be.

She was completely alone, however this changed when she realized she could hear the sound of footsteps heading up the forest behind her. She could make out the silhouette of a single person who had stopped and was just standing there although this wasn't particularly unusual. It still didn't feel quite right so she told herself that it would be best if she kept moving. But as deep as she was going, the dizzier she was feeling. She stopped at a point to drink some water. She was feeling hungry now, so she set off to find an area to camp for the night. As night fell over the forest, the temperature dropped quickly. Fortunately, she managed to set up her tent as soon as she could. A campfire in which she cooked her dinner. She then sat and relaxed thinking deeply into the fire as she reflected on the day that had just gone and excitedly pondered the next journey ahead of her.

She soon retired to the tent and was asleep within minutes through the efforts of the day. The forest was at no time. Completely silent. There are dozens of nocturnal animals and due to this at night the forest comes alive with the sound of insects and marsupials. She felt quite comfortable sleeping to these sounds of nature and felt there were nothing particularly out of the ordinary until she was awoken by the sound of what she thought was crying. She heard it clear even she was in a deep sleep. Clearly undisturbed by this unsettling sound. She then sat up and opened the tent door ever so slightly in order to see if she might be able to discover where the crying was coming from. She was frozen with fear when she realized that a woman in white was sitting in opposite direction of her tent. Not even such far from the tent.

She decided to be silent until she figured out what to do next. She lay there silently in the dark for several minutes listening to the woman whispering and crying. And slowly the crying subsided. She opens her tent door little slightly again to see if the woman is still there or not. The woman wasn't there anymore. So, she stepped out of the tent and said,

"***Hello***"

"***Who are you***?"

"***Are you lost***"?

She got no reply.

However, she was terrified and didn't want to confront any ghost or spirit all by herself alone at scary night. So, she returned to sleep in the tent and slept through undisturbed until the next morning when she relayed the events of the night.

"Who that woman would be doing in this dark forest all by herself"?

"And why she was crying, though?"

Obviously, she had no answers to all that questions. But she was scared. So scared that even in the morning she had to gather her courage to come outside of the tent.

Now she had a new journey ahead, and luckily, she has passed the night resting, otherwise she would have to be sleep all day. And that's not fair to travel all night alone and sleep all day. She started her journey. The forest was beautiful. She could have stopped to spend some time in that beauty but she knew that she was already one night behind.

Who knows that if she could have travelled through the night, she could have found the house? But it was okay to give our body some rest. She was walking and just walking. In the day time the forest isn't scary at all. All the sound she hearing was birds chirping. No wild animals. She travelled all day and now again the sun dropped once again and the night fall. She decided not to stop by for the camp. The more she would rest the more she would be late. She lit her flashlight. She heard someone howling near to her. Probably the wolf. She was stepping silently so the animals cannot track her location. Now she was hearing the sound of someone walking behind her again. But this time she didn't care. She sped up her legs and finally, she saw a house so she gathered her courage and run straight for the house.

She was on the door. There was no any other house, except that one. That '***Lady's house***'. She was living alone.

Diana knocked on the door...

"Knock…knock... (silent...no answer from inside)"

(Meanwhile, there were a lot of terrible voices from that forest.)

She knocked again… ***"Knock…knock..."***

"Is anyone inside?" "Diana asked stridently"

"Please help me" "Knock… knock"

"I need help" "Diana shouted"

"Wait I'm coming... "Someone answered from inside"

"Someone opened the door"

A thought just merged inside Diana's mind, *"how she would look like?" Must have scary face. How am I going to face her? But I don't have any other options. I need her help so I have to face her."*

"Sorry, didn't hear you" *"The lady opened the door"*

Indeed, a beautiful lady was standing there in front of her. Completely opposite of what she was thinking about.

"What are you doing here in the dark night of this nightmarish forest?" "The lady asked"

"I need your help" "Diana requested"

"Come inside, breathing outside is dangerous for you. "The lady offered"

Diana entered her house and breathed for a while until it made her relax.

"Wait, let me make some tea for you. You must have been cold out there" "The lady said"

"Thank you, miss..." "Diana wholehearted appreciated"

"Scarlett, my name is Scarlett" "The witch corrected with a smile"

"Who are you dear? Why did you come to me? I'm a Witch, not an ordinary person to whom you can visit anytime." "Scarlett asked when she served the tea"

“I'm Diana. My home is few miles away from here. And I came here long way only to meet you. I need your help.” “Diana replied”

“What help do you need me with?” “Scarlett asked”

“I need your help in order to teach me the pure secrets of black magic” “Diana answered”

“Who told you, that I teach ‘Black Magic’ to People” “Scarlett asked”

“No. No one told me. I know that you don't. But I also know that you are a witch. And only you can help me this. In this whole world. Can you help me?” “Diana asked”

“But how can I help you, dear?” “Scarlett asked”

“I am born undesired, unholy, and ugly. Everyone hates me. Hates the presence of me. makes fun of me. Says that I’m a cursed. They say that God has abandoned me and no one wants to see me around. Everyone believes that I’m a cursed soul. The demolisher. But I don't want to live like this. I never wanted a life like this. I want to be happy and gorgeous” “Diana replied”

“Oh dear, you're already so pretty. Don’t think this in a negative way. God made you different from others, you're unique. You're the angel. Don't choose yourself according to what other people want you to be” “Scarlett said”

“But I can't bear the agony of my soul, when people laugh at me, say bad things behind my back, make fun of me. My father thinks I’m unfortunate for him…. I can't live my life like this. It's better to die rather than to live in a constant pain. The pain of a cursed life” “Diana started sobbing silently”

“This is not a curse, and do not focus on what people say. Sorry, my child but I can’t help you cause’ you’re not diseased. This is a natural belonging and I can’t do anything about it. It’s against the rule of nature.” “Scarlett answered”

“No, it’s not. People use stuff to treat themselves, their lives. A magic is for a great purpose doesn’t count on bad side. You can use black magics on me. It’s you, and only you. I beg you for this. No one can help me on this. It’s only in your hands?” “Diana asked”

“Listen to me dear, these witchcrafts are Satan's counterfeit stew, and an unholy spirituality. God never endorse those who saturates such practices. The one who practices divination or sorcery interprets omens, engages in witchcraft or casts spells or who is a medium or spiritism or who consults with the dead, is detestable to the Lord. God takes witchcraft very seriously. The penalty for practicing witchcraft under the Mosaic law is death.

Using illicit possessions can open us up to the invasion of demonic spirits engaging in a practice or taking a substance to achieve an altered state of consciousness is a form of witchcraft. There are only two sources of spiritual power God and Satan. Satan has only the power that God allows him to have but it is considerable. To seek spirituality, knowledge or power apart from God is idolatry, closely related to witchcraft. Witchcraft is Satan's realm and he excels in countering what God does. Witchcraft is the desire to know the future, to make them fit better, and to control events that are not ours. To control those abilities, belong only to the Lord. These desires have their roots and Satan's first temptation to Eve. You can't be like God" "Scarlett answered"

"But what about you. Why do you use witchcraft then? Why you disobeyed all those rules" "Diana asked"

"I am a sorcerer. Not a witch. I don't witchcraft, yet I perform magics. I have always treated diseased people by using things grown to nature. Although, I have a complete knowledge of the art of witchcraft but I have never used it for my own benefit or to harm anyone. Witchcraft plays with your mind. It makes you greedy for more and more. It never stops. And a witchcraft, always seek sacrifice. Sorcerer are in the list of those who will not inherit eternal life, those who practice magic arts not for the bad, but for the good, and are the idolaters. And everyone who loves and practices falsehood is not forgivable. We don't need to fear Satan's power but we should respect it and stay away from it. Witchcraft has its many counterparts that promise spirituality, but lead only to emptiness and death only.

Sorcery is the use of spells and magic, speaking to spirits, and divination.

"When you will come into the contact of Satan, there shall not be anyone among you who want his son or his daughter pass through the fire, or one who practices witchcraft, or a soothsayer, or one who interprets omens, or a sorcerer, or one who conjures spells, or a medium, or a spiritisms, or one who calls up the dead. For all who do these things are an abomination to the God, and because of these abominations, God has to punish them out even from their graves. God hates sorcery, and any works like it because they are evil in his sight."

"If you practiced soothsaying, used witchcraft and sorcery, and consulted mediums and spiritisms to see how much evil in the sight of the Lord, to provoke him to anger." And because of how evil it is, God is angry at those who perform such acts. If we do not speak according to what God says, it is because there is no light in us.

People call me a witch. But that is not true. I'm master in sorcery, but in the right way. I know all the rules. And I do not beg for selfishness. I cure diseased people at my best, and I'm afraid you're not sick, my darling" "Scarlett said"

"Then what kind of magic do you perform?" "Diana asked"

"When people visit me and tell me about their pain and sufferings, I use my best knowledge to help them. I repeat here, I help them not change them. I do not go against the law of nature. But I do stand against the evil.

"But I can want whatever I want from witchcrafts" "Diana said"

"It does the job and gives us what we want from the devil, but the devil takes much more in return. God said we shouldn't listen to or follow the devil. The devil also has the power to perform what seems to be miracles and wonders, but that's not what it's all about. It's all about remaining loyal to our Almighty God, and remaining and trusting in him. It's a test, as the Bible teaches, and we can pass his tests by remaining obedient to his commandments. Even when times get tough, we have to stick to what is right. Even when there is an easier way out, we stick with our Almighty God. If we have to endure, if we have to suffer, we don't give in to what is wrong. The Holy Scriptures says those who trust in our Almighty God will abide forever, they are the ones who will inherit the everlasting life in his glorious kingdom. Now, that is something that no one else can give. Not even the devil" "Scarlett answered"

"If God has not given us those blessings, it means that we are not entitled to them all. We don't deserve them and we have no right to achieve it in some other way. If you'll go against the rule of nature, I'm sorry but the impact must be bad. Don't try to step inside of this. It seems so powerful from inside, but from outside it's so dangerous. And most important things, It's against God. Stay away from that child. That's not your business dear. You'll feel so powerful when you have it, but that power will dominate you and one day your voracity will become your faintness, and it will completely abolish you" "Scarlett said"

Even after pleading for her a million times, the sorceress did not agree, because she didn't want to defy nature's rule erroneously.

Diana left there, and now she was going through the motion of disappointment. She swore to herself, that she would learn black magic on her own. She went back home.
"What happened" "Mother asked"

“I met her, but she had no cure for me” “Diana answered”
“Well, this can’t be true” “Mother replied”
“She said she has no cure but she told me the way to cure it myself and I will start thinking upon it” “Diana answered”
“Very well than. Do whatever you want I won’t interrupt, sweetheart” “Mother answered”
She spent several days thinking about what’s wrong or right. But the gluttony was already dominated her. She started living in her room alone. Decided what she have to do. She decided for herself. And her decision was unchanged now. She started collecting candles, making voodoo dolls, pentagram, and other things exactly mentioned on that book. She started reading, learning, and experiencing the ways of black magic from the book and her experiments began as same as it was described in the book. She was now spending her the whole day and night to learn the secrets of it. She didn’t let anyone see what she was doing alone in her room, nor she let anyone enters her room. She used to lock her doors and windows as long as she practices. She was supposed to use black magic on a person who is going to die in some days anyway, who was counting on his last breath. This will not harm anyone in any way. At least that was what she supposed to do.

It took her about one year to learn the recipes, but not completely. She learned only the basics of that. Enough to cure herself but in the darkest ways. She ignored all the words Scarlett warned her about.

She wanted to be pretty. And as mentioned, she had to steal the beauty of someone else. Someone young. And for this purpose, she made those voodoo dolls. She decided her gluttony. The only way to get it was to steal it. Steal it from the others. Because this was the only way that would happen without giving anything of her in return. And of course, she didn't even think about anyone when it came to her own determination. She collected the hairs of some young pretty girls and cast-off black magic to steal her desirables. She selected 9 girls. A little bit of her beauty from each. So, her satanism remains unknown.

Days followed by days and months followed by months, she changed. Beautiful, of course. People didn't figure what really happened with her. A miracle or something else? But everyone's mind got blown when they saw her. But no one couldn't identify how this miracle suddenly happened to her? Some people thought, it should be her aging effect. That she's growing beautiful. But some of them doubted, how did she become so beautiful in such a sudden? Diana was really happy. Now she had all what she wanted.

CHAPTER 6
THE DARK SIDE OF HER

Impressed by what she done, the hard work, didn't take too long to transform her greed into her needs. Wishing for more, she wanted a beauty that could fit into her need. She wanted beauty in perfection. And she chose that path Scarlett warned her about.

Diana crossed the human line because her voracity pushed her to the breaking point. All of the people she trusts to help her to be a good-looking girl made her into a demanding sovereign who will not listen to anyone else. All of the people she hated by, made her into a severe curse, which will not listen to anyone else. Some people are born cursed, and put people in danger with their actions. There is a line that each person has that defines who they are with their revenge, and once a person has crossed that line, they can no longer go back to the person they used to be.

Diana did everything to make herself perfect. People were startled by what they are actually looking at. Unbelievable. That was not a human could do. No miracle happened and if it did, why only on Diana? But some people shrugged it off by saying it, "***the grace of God***."

But that wasn't true at all. She forgot, that she'll use black magic only to cure herself. But she started doing more. She now started worshipping ***'the devil'***. She wanted them to pay for what they done to her when she was the one, they rejected before.

She wanted to be like Scarlett. A powerful sorcerer that could do anything. The one who can make people beg in front of her for help. So, she followed the procedures. The procedure of eating ***'souls of the innocent'***.

One more year has been passed and she was already and almost become master in her field. She became a cruel angel. She started haunting people's soul. The souls of the innocents to become a powerful witch. A powerful witch so she can tell the world that she is the expertise and help them for what they wanted. She wanted to be the most powerful witchcraft magician ever had in history.

She decided to make herself a house, in the forest. In the middle of it. So, she made them believed, including her parents that she wants to live like a monk so she can learn the recipe by herself to treat people like a doctor. No one doubted on her cause' they all believed that she was *'the grace of God, not a curse.'* Even some people helped her build that house. But they didn't know her intentions that she was waiting to haunt. For the innocent souls.

Her mother had no idea what she was onto. She was happy that her daughter is not a curse upon anyone.

And one day…

It was an evening. The sun was already have settled down. But few children were still in the forest, collecting fire sticks for their home. It was known to be no wild animals live there in that forest so was nothing to afraid of. But something was there, about what they were unaware of. Something vicious that had already laid its eyes on them. A sound that whispered in their ears. Summoning them. They were all frozen straight, listening to that voice. Then a few moments later they all started to walk. Followed by the voice that made them whispered too...

I'm going to Diana. Let's play the game of train...

I'm going to Diana. She's calling my name...

I'm going to Diana. She would kill all of my pain...

I'm going to Diana. She'll eat my soul and it's so insane...

They were no longer under control of themselves. Doing what Diana was summing them to do. They were possessed.

Those children never return home. Their parents started to panic when they couldn't find their children. No clues, no footprints, nothing. Nowhere to be found. People didn't have any idea what happened to them, where they went missing. Villagers tried to search for them for weeks, but even after trying so hard, they returned hopeless, but those children never found. They searched for the body thinking if any wild animal could have got him. But there was no dead body either. They asked Diana if she had saw them walking in the woods further, but Diana refused. They believed her and returned back to their places.

Few Weeks Later

One night. Actually, it was midnight. A group of people ware coming back to their home as they live out of their hometown. Four men. They decided their way through that dense forest. The path was dangerous and dark and they did not know that few children were already been missing and no one knows what happened to them. And they could reach their home a little sooner. During their journey, they saw the house. Diana's house, but wasn't there before when they left few months ago. The house was new but they felt something wrong about that. Someone was at the door. Wasn't doing anything. Frozen at the door. Standing still. Either it was waiting for someone to open the door but something was unclear. So, they decided to take a closer look. They went close to it to find out what's wrong with that person. As they approached, it went inside. They asked to wait, but it wasn't listening to them at all.

"Do we have to go inside and check?" "A man asked"

"Let's check" "Another answered"

As they entered, they found the hallway empty. So, they stepped ahead to find more. They saw glimpse of someone going down to the basement, so they followed it. In that basement it was stinking when they saw a boy lying on the floor. He was dead. Searching for more, they found another three children's body lying over the floor. Dead, and someone was standing beside them. Diana. She attacked one of them and inhaled all of her soul into her. It was miserably awful to see his soul coming out and taking space in Diana's. It was such a terrifying, so devastating, that no one can ever imagine. At one moment she was eating then in the next, she turned around. Turned her face towards them, such a cruel face.

They still couldn't believe that Diana was doing that to those innocent children. The moment they realized that it's not a safe place to stay still, they just started to run. But she was a creepy witch now. Just as they ran back to the village, she ran after them. She chased those people to eat their souls too, but they thrived in saving their lives by running as fast as they could. It was such a terrifying incident they've ever imagined their entire life.

When they reached the village, they told everyone about her, about the children that she killed months ago. They told her what she now became, what she did to them. The wrath filled inside of them so they decided to search her house at the first light. They felt guilt thinking about how fool they were, and how could they have believed her, calling her 'grace of God' instead of 'the devil's child.'

CHAPTER 7
THE DEATH OF RISE

It was early morning when Diana's mother heard poundings on her door. She panicked but she was cooking so she called Diana to answer the door. But Diana didn't show up so she got to the door to see who was there pounding. The priest and all the people from her neighbourhood was there. She afraid what was wrong. So, she asked, curiously.

"What happened, father?" "Diana's mother asked"

"Where is your daughter?" "Priest asked"

"In her room, I believe" "Diana's mother answered"

"Let's go" "Priest said"

"Wait, what's happening? Anybody, please tell me" "Diana's mother requested"

"Where's the witch" "A man asked"

"What? Who? What witch?" "Diana's mother asked"

"Your daughter" "A man replied"

"Don't you dare to call her that. She's my daughter, not a witch" "Diana's mother shouted"

"Let's find out" "The man said"

They said and went to check the house.

"She's not here" "Priest said"

"I think we know, where she could be. The house we built for her, in the forest" "The man said"

"Very well. Lets' go than" "Priest said"

When they reached there, the house was locked from inside.

"Break it" "Priest ordered"

They break the door. And there she was.

It was stinking when they all broke the door, but shocked. Shocked to see her that way. She was in the middle of her witchcraft. Praying to demon. They found that sigil of Baphomet painted on the wooden floor which was basically the sign of Satan. Around it was a bunch of freaky voodoo dolls. But from where this stink was coming from? They searched the whole house. And they found everything in the basement what they have been looking for. The rotting corpses of the missing children she kept under her basement.

“Look what you’ve done, sweetheart” “Priest said”

“Diana? What are you doing here?” “Diana’s mother asked”

“Don’t you see? It’s black magic. She’s into witchcraft. Worship of the devil” “A man answered”

“Why are you doing this, my daughter?” “Diana’s mother asked”

She’s not your daughter. Not anymore. She became a witch now. A greedy, cruel and hungry witch” “Priest answered”

“Forgive her. Please forgive her. She won’t do it again” “Diana’s mother requested”

“This wouldn’t happen again. Tie her hands, and take her with us.” “The priest sad”

"Let me go, I promise I will not do anything like it again"
"Diana was screaming"
"You have already done a lot" "Priest replied"
While repeating the interiors, Priests kept some firewood under her feet. They first sprinkled holy water on her body. She was about to be burn.
"Please forgive her, at least for once. Give her a chance to remorse" "Her mother begged"
"Go and check her house's basement. You'll know better what she done behind your knowledge, beneath your nose" "A man said"
"Last night she was about to kill me too, unfortunately for her, I escaped" "The man said"
"If I would've been strong enough, I could've stopped her. But I never knew about all these stuffs she was into" "Her mother said crying"
"Please let me go. I will not do anything from now on I swear. I promise to everyone" *"She was screaming, praying and pleading, but no one was listening to her"*
"You are a witch and you have to die. Just like you killed our children" "The crowd were shouting at her"
She was tied with a dead tree and a man struck a fire on the ground to her feet. The crowd can feel the shush of the flames against the skin of their faces. Then a low, wet,

chewing sound, a sound like a hive of insects eating and eating, as the fire feeds on the pile of refuse. They could see her burning body. She was screaming, like an innocent little girl. Crying out of her death. The fire that was slowly burning her body and the pain that was she going through was insufferable.

Her mother who couldn't bear of pain to see her burning and dying daughter in front of her eyes, unconsciously fell on the ground. The anger and emptiness in the eyes of those who lost their beloved children were screaming on their faces. The rage of unforgiveness.

After few moments, she suddenly stopped screaming. Completely silent now. Dead. Her body was down into ashes. But those people who punished her, did not have that fulfillment in their eyes even after she was burnt to death. And they knew, deep down, that their children and beloved ones were never going to come back no matter what they do to her.

Everything was finished and silent now. Came to an end. The crowd, the place, the screenings. Stopped.

"Did everyone get what they wanted? Did that make everyone happy?" "Diana's father asked"

Then he wiped his tears, carried his wife and walked away from the crowd to leave the place forever and to never come back.

A few moments later after he left, the crowd felt some movements. Movements in Diana's ashes. Her ashes were gradually spinning around, like a little tornado near to the ground. Then the spinning sped up and rose vertically to form a real tornado. A huge one. The crowd was scared and was like, 'What's happening?" Before they could understand it, the soul of Diana's walked out of the whirling ashes, screaming…

"***Listen to me villagers, I'm cursing you all***"

I'll return to meet, wander in those streets,

You would weep when I start eating you deep,

I'll eat your souls and put you into deep sleep,

You'll beg for your life, But I would be your darkest dream…

And she vanished.

Before something more would happen, they collected and imprisoned her remains and her black book with a spell cast with their own blood... to ensure that Diana's dark power would never be found. And that is why she has been stricken

from the chronicles. This evil was now bound to remain frozen for eternity. They named it, ***"The Grave of Diana."***
"*In the name of God, I command you, you are Diana a witch, will be imprisoned forever and will not be able to harm any innocent in this village"* "AMEN" "Priests prayed"

The door was locked by a holy incantation, sealed by a red cloth, and advised to not to break the seal. "If anyone does, then its soul would free, and it would not let anyone live."

CHAPTER 8
BRING BACK MEMORIES

A few years later, a group of 4 men, 26 to 29 years old, were hiking through a forest they never encountered before. This new path led them to this unknown forest as they already lost their lead. Unaware of what this forest been through. Didn't care, they were just trespassing through, but in the middle of the night. They all have already been walking for a long, long time. They've been walking, walking and walking, in hope of a shelter to stay for the night, but still hadn't found anything yet. As a matter of fact, it was strange how they were walking without any fear inside of them. But finally, they finally saw a house at the end of the dark forest after walking for so long. It was a cold night outside and they had no other option rather than to stay there and wait for the morning to shine. But they were unaware of the nightmare that awaits them.

The house was old and creepy. Abandoned for so long. Seemed like it was going to be fall in any minute. As they moved their steps onward to that house, something shined. Like someone lit the lantern. But how is it possible? The house was so old like it's been abandoned for years and can be isolate any minute. And the most important thing, how someone can live there. This house is a death trap.

"Whoa! Did you see that?" "A man asked"

"I think someone is still in this house. We can ask for help" "Another man said"

When they poached to the main door, they were surprised to see that the door was locked by a red cloth but was easy to untie. And there were some incantations on the door, behind the weeds that have been overgrown on it.

"I think there is something wrong. I'm not feeling good for going inside" "A man said"

"We don't have another option. Let's check inside, really quick. And if we feel something wrong, we'll run back out" "Another man said"

They broke the seal and entered the house. The house was creepy and so empty. No one was there. No lantern, nothing at all. It was awfully dark inside. They lit the flashlight and started to shine in every corner of that house.

"Hello? Is someone here?" "A man asked"

As they tried to get inside the lights turned on. A lady was there.

"How can I help you?" "The lady asked"

"Hey. Sorry, we don't want to disturb you. We all are hikers, were hiking through this forest but we were walking from so long and that made us tired so we just want a roof above us to rest. Only for the night" "A man answered"

"Where you all heading up, in such a dreadful night? Don't you know about the witch ghost?" The lady asked"

"What, no, we never heard anything about her. We're just trespassers. Strangers u can say. Everything is here is new for us and so this forest. We lost our lead and enter this way. Then we saw your house, and thought if we can spend the night here. Would be safer than sleeping out in the woods, right?" "A man said and laughed a little"

"She's evil. She kills everyone she saw in the night. You were lucky that she didn't find you" "The lady answered"

"Seriously? Oh my God" "A man asked"

"Yes. I live upstairs. You can use the hallway to spend rest of your night. But I want you all to leave with the first light in the morning" "The lady answered"

“Don’t worry madam, we will. Thank you so much for this kindness” “The man answered”

It was around 3 o'clock when one of them suddenly awoken by some strange noise. But he couldn’t see anything as the room was so dark. Waited for few more minutes, then went back to sleep when he heard nothing more after all. Few more minutes passed when he again heard the same strange noise coming in his ears. But this time, it was closer than it was before. He slowly searched for his flashlight and shine to find for the noise. He got his spirit trembled when he turned his head back around to check on his friends. The lady was there, eating the soul of one of his friends. Her mouth was opened so big, eyes were burning, and hairs were floating up in the air.

The soul was leaving out of his friend’s body and inhabiting the space inside the lady. As he checked, another two were lying on the floor. Already dead. And the last were now dead too. Empty from inside. And now, it's his turn to die.

“You were the witch ghost” “He murmured to himself and ran”

He tried to run away as fast as he could, but she was so fast and powerful that he couldn't make his escape possible.

She ate his soul too, and now, she was free. And it was the time for the villagers to pay what she promised.

CHAPTER 9
THE WRATH OF HER

She was very quiet and reserved but dreads the situation. She tries to make it look like she had nothing to do with the decision when in reality it was her fulfillment. She tells people very quietly that "you have to see me do this," effectively telling them that she is the only one they will follow.

It became like a disaster so far, cause' she started killing people of that village every day. She started from the people who voted to burn her first. That house became the most haunted house in that village. She'll not stop until a single person of that village was alive. She was killing at least 2 people every day.

Diana was one of the people cursed by Gods, but this was before her death. Now she has become like a ruthless victory over innocent people. As the show progresses, everyone learns that the village is going to end. They have a bunker but only so many people can live there. There is a fight to the death between her and the villagers and even after that, there will be no survivors.

She eats them alive from the fighting pits that were set up for the soul to fight their way out of punishment. And that was going as smoothly as she expected. A flashback through her eyes, effectively making her the worse.

A couple of weeks passed, Diana was daily haunting the people and was becoming stronger every day. Priests of that village did their best to get rid of that ghost, but no one can't even able to stand in front of her strength. The last person she kills was a man who stands up in fear to try and leave the situation because he knows if he opposes her, he will die. Diana killed him anyway because not following what she said when she was burning was a direct threat and attack to her. She wanted to shut down anything that had already possibly hurt her. She tells everyone that there's no escape. They have to face the monster they created.

She becomes a dreadful ghost with no emotions.

Diana vanished the whole village in less than a year. And now she was on search for the migrated ones.

(The night Isabella's parents died)

It was the witching hour and they were sleeping. All of a sudden Isabella's mother woke up after some strange howling sound. She saw someone right in front of her. Staring at her. Dark black shadow, glowing red eyes, floating hairs. She tried to wake up Isabella's father and pointed towards the ghost. But before they could understand or act anything, she swallowed both of their souls in a moment. The last word that came out from Isabella's mother's mouth was, please.

Now Diana has become an invincible, cruel, and dreadful ghost. Cause' now, she has only one person left to haunt…... and that was Isabella.

CHAPTER 10
THE GRAVE

I'm going to die. And I'm unable to cleanse myself off my thoughts of fears and death that is following me from ages. What am I going to do? Watch myself die? I'm an easy kill. She killed so many people, along with the people of God. What am I supposed to do now? And why you never told me about this Auntie?" "I asked"

"Your mother knew everything, but she never wanted you to live in a constant fear of death behind you. She wanted to protect you" "Aunt Hadley said"

"But what about you, how did she spare you" "I asked curiously"

“I was your mother’s half-sister. We’re not connected with bloodline, but with the heart. A connection more than any bloodline between two sisters could. We were more than sisters. She loved me and cared me like a mother. For a younger sibling like me, she was a guardian to me. But she never took credit for that” “Aunt Hadley answered”

“And what about my father? Was his bloodline…?” “I asked”

“Yes. Your grandfather was young, and your father was a little boy when it all happened in that village, and so your mother’s father too. It was before I was introduced to your family. They both were connected to the same point, unfortunately.” “Aunt Hadley answered”

“How you met my mother?” “I asked”

“I was 5, when I first saw her. My father died when I was two years old. Later on, your mother’s father married my mother and adopted me. So technically I didn’t belong to the same bloodline” “Aunt Hadley answered”

“That means she recognises every bloodline that she cursed that day. But what happened to Diana’s parents?” “I asked”

“They both are dead, few years later as they couldn’t handle the guilt and pain they were breathing through. Diana knows that she is the reason behind her parents’ death, and that made her even more of a filthy vicious ghost” “Aunt Hadley answered”

“That means there’s nowhere to go. Nowhere to escape. I’m going to die anyway” “I said grievingly”

“No. I don’t think so” “Aunt Hadley said”

“But what made you think that. There’s nothing we can do here, Aunt Hadley” “I said”

“The witch of the forest. Maybe she could help you” “Aunt Hadley answered”

“Who?” “I asked doubting”

“The one who declined Diana’s request” “Aunt Hadley answered”

“But how could it be possible. She must’ve died a decade ago.” “I answered”

“Keep in mind that she is a witch, and witches don’t die so early” “Aunt Hadley answered”

“And she is my only hope, and I have got only one chance” “I said”

“Yes.” “Aunt Hadley answered”

“Can I borrow your car, Auntie?” “I asked”

“Yes, of course darling. But I’m coming too” “Aunt Hadley said”

“No auntie, I can’t put your life in danger too.” “I answered”

“Sweetheart, be safe. You are the only one left to me” “Aunt Hadley said”

“I promise, Auntie” “I answered”

The next morning, I started the car and drove about 70 miles north. From a highway, I steer inside to a village described on the map which was leading into the forest on a pretty desolate road to get there. I had to drive down the twisted and seemingly abandoned road. After driving for hours, I finally saw a house alone in the forest. I left my car there, and hiked down a windy path.

I knew someone had to be there. But the road was calm and scary at night. I had a flashlight, and I began to walk forward into the trees. It was completely pitch black anywhere and the light was not shining. Walking through the darkness completely not expecting what will happen next. I was by myself surrounded by darkness and trees.

I stumbled in one direction and then another and then fell down. I sat up alone and then looked up into the trees. I could see the tops of them and the stars in the sky.

My gaze was cut short when I heard the footsteps approaching me. I looked in the direction of the twigs crunching below my feet but saw only the figure of someone and talked to myself.

"I need to carry myself back"

The shadow continued walking to me and I tried to focus on her sight but I could only see the outline of that shadow. The feeling of sobriety hit me and I knew that I'm in real danger. But after immediately I stood up and began running away. I started running toward that house. I was running efficiently, but as I ran, I heard someone running behind me. I know that she was with me. This feeling, I already know this feeling already. Like I'm already in this before. But where?

Yes, the dream. I remembered it. The nightmare that comes to me every night. And that nightmare came into reality. This feeling of get known hit my soul and shivered my body. Everything was exactly the same I dreamt of. So, I sped up my legs and pounded on the door.

“Please... Please help me... let me in.

“Is anyone home? Please help me...” “I screamed”

“Wait for me, I'm coming...” “Scarlett answers from inside”

As soon as Scarlett opened the door, I entered in such a frightening way and closed the door behind me immediately.

“What happened, dear? Who are you? And what are you doing in this forest on such a howling dark night? What made you scared? A bear, a wolf, or what?” “Scarlett questioned shockingly”

“Someone or something was after me. It was dark. A dark shadow, chasing me, running behind me, hungry for me...” “I answered with frightening”

“Don't worry dear, you are now safe inside. No one can harm you. Just calm down. Take a deep breadth and then you could tell me what took you here” “Scarlett encouraged”

“Ma’am, can you please help me? Can you please tell me how to kill that witch ghost?” “I trembled”

“What witch? I didn’t understand” “Scarlett asked”

“Everyone knows about the ghost of that witch. She killed everyone and now she’s after me. I'm the last one remaining for her to finish and she won't make it delay” “I answered”

“Hold on, take a deep breath, and just calm down and then explain it to me. “Scarlett encouraged me and went to the kitchen for some water”

“I drank the whole glass of water and started explaining”

“Diana, the witch. The girl who was burnt by the villagers for the things she done. She is now returned and she’s after me” “I answered”

“Yes, I know about her. I know her from the beginning when she came to me because she wanted help. But then I felt the dark intentions in his eyes that surrounded her innocent soul. So, I declined her request and warned her to stay away from this black magic thing. But she didn’t stop.

A vengeful ghost or **vengeful spirit** is said to be the spirit of a dead person who returns from the afterlife to seek revenge for a cruel, unnatural or unjust death. And I’m afraid, she won’t stop until she completes what she has promised. ‘The curse’. But maybe I have a way to escape. Maybe we can make her go. But I’m not completely sure”

“Scarlett said hopefully”

“Oh my God, I think… I think she’s around us. I can sense her. I can feel her” I interrupted her”

“She’s dead and stronger enough to turn herself into an immortal. She will follow her victims. She wants to stab everyone to death, eat their souls, and free them from this

world for her curse. She won't stop until she takes out every part of your soul inside of her.
Listen to me carefully, dear, I'm unable to fight with that witch, I'm old now and she became so powerful that I can't stand in front of her, even I know that she can't haunt me because I'm not the part of her curse. But still, I can't fight her. If I do, she will kill me too in her aggression that I couldn't help her when she needed me the most. But if you can sense her, that means you can fight her. I can show you the way but you have to fight on your own.

Keep your faith inside of your heart. God is with you because he says “I will come near you for judgment. I will be a swift witness Against sorcerers”
And his judgment is, “the cowardly, unbelieving, abominable, murderers, sorcerers, idolaters, and all liars shall have their part in the lake which burns with fire and brimstone, which is the second death”.
It means you still have a chance to kill her again. Yeah, it’s possible cause’ she defied God’s rule and now her soul is entitled to it. Chronicles tells us that soul died because it was unfaithful to the Lord. It didn’t keep the word of the Lord and even consulted a medium for guidance in the New Testament.

You have to go to that house where she once used to do her witchcrafts. The house, where her dark side was born and grew up. That haunted house near Millwood village. You have to burn her grave along with her witchcrafts lying beneath her house and the most important thing, her black magic book, which she used to learn black magics.

Here, take this, it will help you and prevent you from that witch ghost. You have to spread it all over her face if she appeared to you. Make sure you burn her everything with this holy water. Otherwise, she will haunt you till death"

"Scarlett gave the holy water to me and said"

"God will help you because you haven't done anything bad to her, it was those people who burnt her and participated themselves in her curse. But keep in your mind, whatever happens, don't be afraid.

Don't be afraid even if she is standing in front of you, making eye contact with you. You must have to convince her that you don't fear her. May God give you the strength to fight her, bless you and have mercy with you" "Scarlett said and gave every essential that I would need soon."

I left Scarlett's house with her blessings and lots of courage. Ignited my car to the road that would lead to that haunted house of that witch ghost. I drove for about 15 minutes, and far about 6 miles later, the road ended. The car has been reached to its limits. I had to walk all the way to that house alone on foot, so I shut the car down, packed my bag with the things that was going to help me with that. Like matchbox, a can filled with petrol and the most important, that holy water.

CHAPTER 11
THE HOUSE OF HORROR

I was in the forest. It was a zero-moon night, a deserted forest, darkness all around and I was isolated. No sign of human, just horrible voices of wild animals that hides to haunt. The sound of blowing wind was already making the night so scary. I was outfaced and chokehold. I walked down the road which was completely overgrown with weeds and you couldn't even tell that it had once a road. I was just walking and walking… No end.

After walking for a long time, I saw a house, at the end of the road. The house was really old and everything was constantly collapsing. It was the creepiest thing that my eyes laid over. Covered with weeds and it clearly had been abandoned for years. The house looked very uninviting regardless of some encouragement. There must be that village near somewhere. And I could imagine how devastating to see those empty houses after when she killed them all. The whole empty village. The roads, garden, lakes, rooms where they once lived before their soul get eaten by her. I couldn't gather the courage to see the village for myself. I can't imagine what it could be for the people who suffered. The devastation for the innocent one who saw their loved ones dying. The one who never done anything wrong to her. Or the one who wasn't even born when it all happened. All these thoughts just left my heart trembled. I was just getting goosebumps and the fear that continuously pushing be backwards. But I have to do it. And so, I did. I did gather my courage to walk to that house. And when I poached to that house, Diana was there. Standing right in front of the house.

"Why are you just standing there? Come to me and show me your scary face" "I shouted at her without fear"

"I apologize for the delay. I have something I want to ask you. Have you ever put yourself in the middle of nowhere? Wanting to see what is behind those dense trees? What is lurking inside my old house that has been dead and forgotten for years? Have you ever gone so far that you

can't bring yourself to turn back?" "Diana shivered me with her scary voice"

"I'm not afraid of you. I'm not like others. I can sense. I can stand in front of you and can put my eyes directly into yours. You can't eat my soul. You don't have much powers, witch" "I spoke to her"

"I'm the sand in your hand… the vicious not friend,
I see you starting to sweat… I'm' the ice down your back…"
"Diana shivered me again"

And within a second after I completed my words, she was in front of my eyes just in an instant speed. And I was just stunned. Froze, and breathless. Paralysed. Unable to move myself.
"Oh my God, she is so powerful" "I scared myself with my words"
"I can feel your fears in your soul.
"I can feel your soul is too good for me. The taste of victory" "Diana answered"

As she opened her mouth to inhale my soul, I splashed the holy water onto her face and stepped backward. A few yards back.

Diana could not bear the power of that holy water. Her face started to burn, evaporating like water vapours. She started to scream. And for that she disappeared from there for a while. It gave me a little courage to act something more. I quickly ran towards the main door of that house and tried opening the front door.

It opened but not so easily. The foyer was filled with the broken glass and the door was struggling to open over some of the debris. I got it open enough to gain entry, and when I looked around the place, shivers run down through my spine.

There were voodoo dolls, candles, dead skulls in the living room. It was so eerie. The weirdest thing I saw was the corpses of people in that house. There were stairs to the basement, and I had no desire to go down but I had to find the grave of Diana. I lifted my legs and started up the steps. Each step on the old wooden stairs would creak and bend. When I was about halfway down the stairs, I heard what sounded like an animal. The sounds came from downstairs and it sounded like an animal who had just woken up.

I heard it gasp and snarl and then start walking. I had terror on my face. It doesn't sound like a dog or any other animal that could be non-threatening. I took a step down and the wood creek. I froze and my eyes closed as I knew the animal had heard me.

The footsteps of the animal stopped and suddenly I heard whatever it was, running in the direction of the staircase. I spread holy water on myself and slammed my feet fast. The scary sound of that animal stopped. Stopped like it was nothing there. Peaceful but unnerving.

I went down and saw there, the grave of Diana. And her black book placed upon it. I slammed her witchery stuff on her grave without wasting any time and took out the holy water and spread that all over her grave. I had to burn it all and make sure that nothing left, otherwise, the ghost won't let me live.

Trying to lit my matchsticks, as quicker as possible. But it always went wrong when we rushing through it. And the same thing happened, the matchsticks never lit.

And the time came what was beating dread in my heart. She appeared back. I sensed her again. I turned around my head. And I saw her red glowing eyes, staring me from the stairs. The cruel eyes, hungry for my soul. I could see her burnt face by the holy water I splashed on her face. And this time she was more horror to me. And then, she was now steering herself to me. At first, she was slow but then, she sprinted. I had no other option rather than to lit my matchstick or I'm dead. I had only one chance. And for so, I splashed the holy water on her again.

She was screaming again...screaming like a spine-chilling animal.

She had to eat my soul and it would be possible only if she would possess me, but I won't let her do this. I won't let myself die. I was continuously splashing the holy water on her. I splashed holy water one more time on her grave followed by the petrol and lit my matchsticks, tried to burn the book first on fire so I could throw it on her grave. And by the mercy of God, the book catch fire and I throw it on the grave and ran. I had to run from that house really quick, if I didn't, I will be the next who's burning right with her. But she was in the middle of the hallway when I climbed upstairs.

"How am I going to overtake her? She's will catch me with her bare hands. I have only one choice left" "I murmured to myself"

I splashed the last few drops of holy water remaining all over her face but this time, she dodged it.

She dodged it and I had now an empty bottle left in my hand. And a thought came inside my head, "I'm dead now." And she started laughing. Like an old woman laugh. She now knows that she has won the war.

I remembered the words that Scarlet told me, "Keep your faith inside of your heart. God is with you because he says "I will come near you for judgment. I will be a swift witness Against sorcerers."
So, I prayed. Prayed to God if he can help me if I'm innocent. Because it was never me. It was the people who participated in hear death."
And then a miracle happened. Her ashes came in contact with the holy water inside her grave, that made her fell on the floor. She felt it. She felt that power of God. She felt so weak and harmless and screamed. A bloodcurdling scream that could have given me heart attack.
But gathering all my strength and courage I said ***"Watch me burn all the memories of yours"*** and before the ghost could do anything, I drove my feet outside of that house. I locked the door and tied the latch with the same cloth which was tied before by the priests.
The whole house was on fire now, and Diana was crying inside. Screaming like a girl and saying, if there will be any way, I will return to you, under any circumstances to fulfill

my curse. And no one will ever stop me from doing that. You will have to see my return.

And the time came when the whole house went down into ashes. Nothing left. I walked back to my car to leave. Started my car, turn around the steering and accelerated forward. Watching the flaring fire of her basement through my rear mirror. But even while leaving, there was a question in my mind.

"Will she come back for me?"

"YESSSSS" "A soft voice in my ears shivered me"

I stopped the car and turned my eyes all around, but no one was there.

"It must be the fear inside of my head driving me, scaring me" "I murmured to myself, sped up the car, and left that forest.

THE END

THE HOUSE OF A BROKEN SHADOW

A Ghost Story

www.ingramcontent.com/pod-product-compliance
Lightning Source LLC
Chambersburg PA
CBHW062143160726
48282CB00027B/928
* 9 7 8 9 3 3 4 0 7 7 6 8 1 *